The Lost and Found Puppy
by Mary Jane Flynn

Copyright © 1991
Mary Jane Flynn

Published by
Storytellers Ink
Seattle, Washington

ISBN 0-9623072-6-2

Printed in Mexico

Dedicated to Ben

It happened on a lonely road

quite early in the day –

a passing car dropped off a box,

and then just drove away.

The tiny puppy in the box,

who watched without a sound,

kept thinking, "When they see I'm gone,

they'll surely turn around."

And so he sat and waited there,

till finally he knew

that searching for a new home

was the best thing he could do.

He walked along for hours

toward the salty ocean air,

but all the beach seemed empty

by the time that he got there.

"I don't think you belong here,"

said a crab who scuttled by.

"I guess you're right," the puppy said,

and sighed a lonely sigh.

He turned and wandered on

until the beach was far behind.

He traveled on some railroad tracks

he'd happened just to find,

and all was well and quiet,

till a warning whistle blew –

The puppy ran for safety

as a train came into view.

He hid among the bushes

as the train went thundering past,

and crept out very slowly

when it disappeared at last.

He knew he must keep going

for it wasn't long till dark ...

At last the weary puppy

found his way into a park.

Perhaps he'd find a home here,

in the woods so dark and deep.

He curled up in a soft, cool spot

and soon fell fast asleep.

Awakening, he found that he

was faced with a surprise....

"Lossst?" the snake hissed softly,

staring with unblinking eyes.

The puppy jumped up, saying,

"No, I'm sure I'll find my way!"

He hurried on and told himself

he'd rest no more that day.

There wouldn't be much daylight left;

the sun was going down.

He found a path that led him

to the busy part of town.

The streets were filled with traffic,

for the working day was through.

The puppy huddled there alone

while truck and car horns blew.

At last he found the sidewalk

with his heart still beating fast,

but he was nearly trampled

by the people rushing past.

He saw a tiny swinging door

and pushed it open wide.

He went in, hoping it might be

a place where he could hide.

He found himself inside a room

with pets of every kind.

He hadn't been invited in,

but no one seemed to mind.

"There's room here in our shelter,"

they all said. "Why don't you stay?"

The puppy said, "I'd like to

rest a while here, if I may."

ANIMAL
SHELTER

OPEN
9 am–9 pm

A goldfish, blowing bubbles, said,

"There's room in here with me.

You'll love it in the water –

it's the only place to be!"

The puppy learned a lesson

he was sure not to forget:

a puppy in a fish bowl

just feels crowded, cold, and wet.

A bird sang to the puppy,

"You may join me for tonight.

There's room upon my perch,

as long as you don't mind the height."

But clinging to the branch

the puppy learned a few more things.

He learned that puppies do mind heights,

because they don't have wings.

A mother cat purred, "Puppy,

you'd be better off down here."

At last the warm, dry puppy felt

his worries disappear.

The mother cat had offered him

some food from her own dish...

ANIMAL
SHELTER
OPEN
9 am–9 pm

But unlike cats, a puppy HATES

the sight and smell of fish!

Just then the door was opened

by a mother and her child.

The young girl saw the puppy,

and she stepped inside and smiled.

"This shelter is for animals,"

the puppy heard her say,

"who have no one to care for them

and have no place to stay.

We came here hoping we would find

a puppy just like you.

We'll take you back to our home,

which will now be your home, too!"

ANIMAL
SHELTER
OPEN
9 am–9 pm

She held the puppy gently

as she walked across the floor.

He waved goodbye to all his friends

just as they reached the door,

and thought of all the things he'd learned

that he had never known.

He'd found a great deal more

than just a place to call his own...

ANIMAL
SHELTER
OPEN
9 am-9 pm

He'd found someone to love him,

and someone to be his friend.

And so upon a happy note,

this puppy's tale can end.